KU-001-470

yummy

For Jo

First published 2009 by Walker Books Ltd
87 Vauxhall Walk, London SE11 5HJ

2 4 6 8 10 9 7 5 3 1

© 2009 Lucy Cousins

The right of Lucy Cousins to be identified as author/illustrator of this work
has been asserted by her in accordance with the
Copyright, Designs and Patents Act 1988

This book has been typeset in Gill Sans MT Schoolbook.
Handlettering by Lucy Cousins.

Printed in China.

All rights reserved. No part of this book may be reproduced,
transmitted or stored in an information retrieval system
in any form or by any means, graphic, electronic or mechanical,
including photocopying, taping and recording,
without prior written permission from the publisher.

British Library Cataloguing in Publication Data:
a catalogue record for this book is available from the British Library

ISBN 978-1-4063-1621-6

www.walker.co.uk

yummy

Lucy Cousins

WALKER BOOKS
AND SUBSIDIARIES

LONDON • BOSTON • SYDNEY • AUCKLAND

Contents

Little Red Riding

Once upon a time there was

a girl called Little Red Riding Hood.

Her mother asked her to take a

basket of food through the wood

to her grandmother, who was ill.

Hood

Little Red Riding Hood had not gone
far when she met a wolf.
"Where are you going, Little Red
Riding Hood?" the wolf asked.
"I am taking a basket of food to
my grandmother, because she is ill,"
answered Little Red Riding Hood.
"Is that so?" said the wolf with a
nasty grin and away he ran.

13

14

The wolf ran straight to Grandmother's

house and knocked at the door.

"Who's there?" called Grandmother.

"It's me, Little Red Riding Hood," said

the wolf in a sweet little voice. "I've

brought you a basket of food."

"Come in then," said Grandmother.

gulp

The wolf went in, leapt on to
Grandmother's bed and
swallowed her whole.

After a while Little Red Riding Hood arrived at Grandmother's house. She walked straight in and over to the bed.

"Grandmother, what big eyes you have," she said.

"All the better to see you with, my dear," replied the wolf.

"Grandmother, what big ears you have."

"All the better to hear you with, my dear."

"Grandmother, what big teeth you have."

"All the better to eat you with, my dear!"

And with that the wolf leapt out of bed
and gobbled up Little Red Riding Hood.

A hunter was passing and heard the noise. He came in and saw the wicked wolf.

chop

He chopped the wolf open
and out stepped Grandmother
and Little Red Riding Hood.
"HOORAY!" they cried.
Then they ate up the food
in the basket and lived
happily ever after.

21

The three

Billy Goats Gruff

Once upon a time there were three billy goats, Big Billy Goat Gruff, Middle Billy Goat Gruff and Little Billy Goat Gruff. They lived on a hillside by a river. The grass on the far side of the river looked so green that one day they decided to go and eat it. But first they had to cross the bridge, and under the bridge lived a great ugly troll.

First Little Billy Goat Gruff stepped on to
the bridge. TRIP TRAP, TRIP TRAP
went his hooves.

"Who's that tripping over my bridge?"
roared the troll.

"It's me," said Little Billy Goat Gruff in
a very little voice.

"I'm coming to gobble you up," said the troll.

"Oh please don't eat me," said
Little Billy Goat Gruff. "I'm only small.
Wait for the next billy goat, he's much bigger."

"Well, be off with you,"
said the troll.

trip trap

25

Then Middle Billy Goat Gruff stepped on to the bridge.

TRIP TRAP, TRIP TRAP went his hooves.

"Who's that trip-trapping over my bridge?"

roared the troll.

"It's me," said Middle Billy Goat Gruff in a middling voice.

"I'm coming to gobble you up,"

said the troll.

"Oh please don't

eat me," said

Middle Billy Goat

Gruff. "I'm only middle-sized.

Wait for the next billy

goat, he's much bigger."

"Well, be off with you,"

said the troll.

trip
trap

trip trap

Big Billy Goat Gruff stepped on
to the bridge. TRIP TRAP, TRIP TRAP
went his hooves very loudly.
"Who's that stamping over my
bridge?" roared the troll.
"It's me," said Big Billy Goat Gruff
in his great big voice.
"I'm coming to gobble you up,"
said the troll.
"Then I'll bash you to bits,"
said Big Billy Goat Gruff.

28

Big Billy Goat Gruff put down his head and charged at the troll, butting him so hard he flew up into the air and then down into the middle of the river.

The troll was never seen again and the billy goats got so fat eating grass on the far side of the river that they were scarcely able to walk home again.

The enormous turnip

Once upon a time an old man wanted to grow turnips, so he scattered some seeds on his garden and said, "Grow, seeds, grow. Grow into big juicy turnips."

he pulled and

The next morning the old man went out to the garden and found that one enormous turnip had grown. But when he tried to pull it up, he pulled and he pulled but it wouldn't come out.

34

he pulled

The old man called the old woman.

"Please help me pull up the turnip," he said.

The old woman called the boy.

"Please help us pull up the turnip," she said.

The boy called the girl.

"Please help us pull up the turnip," he said.

they pulled and

They pulled and they pulled but the enormous turnip just wouldn't come out.

they pulled

"Dog, Dog, help us pull up the turnip," called the girl.

They pulled and they pulled.

"Cat, Cat, help us pull up the turnip," called the dog.

They pulled and they pulled.

"Mouse, Mouse, help us pull up the turnip," called the cat.

They pulled and they pulled and they pulled ...

they pulled and they pulled

and at last out came the turnip!

They took the turnip
home and chopped it
and cooked it and had

an enormous feast
and they are probably
still eating it now!

Henny Penny

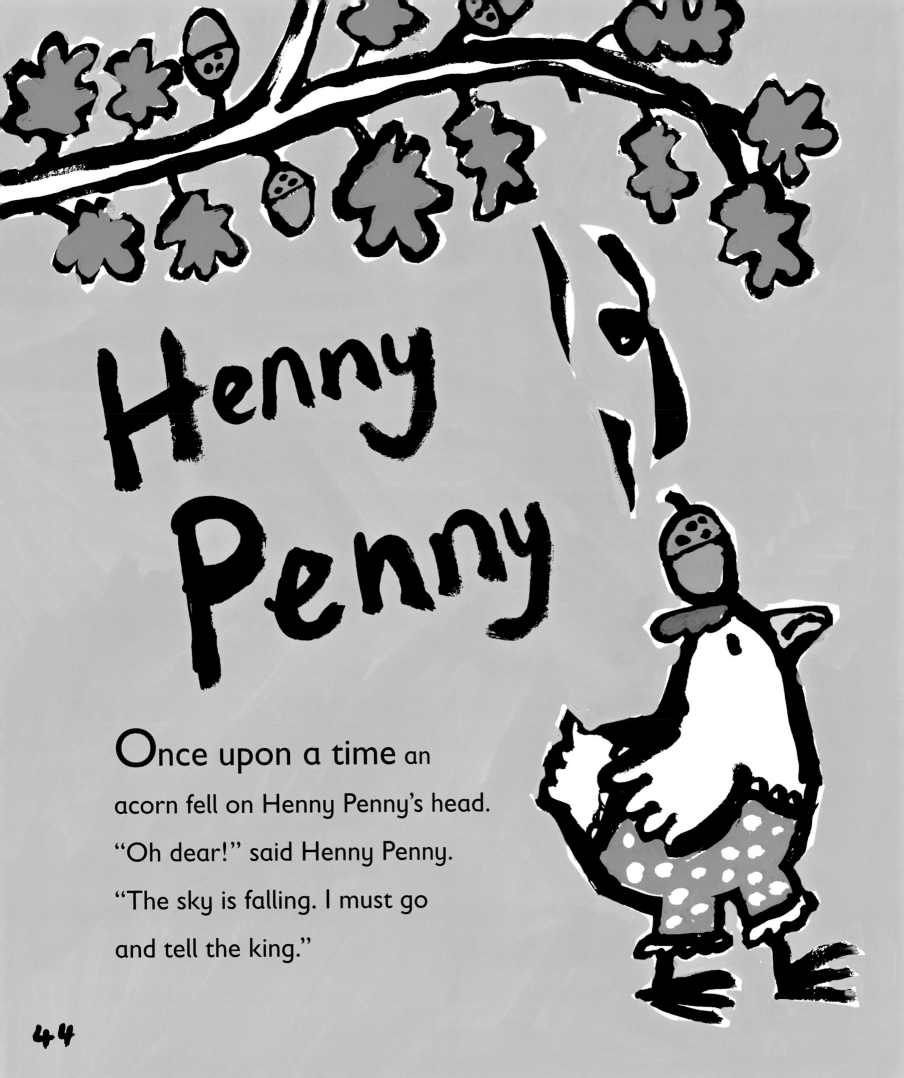

Once upon a time an
acorn fell on Henny Penny's head.
"Oh dear!" said Henny Penny.
"The sky is falling. I must go
and tell the king."

She went along and she went along and soon she met Cocky Locky.

"Where are you going?" asked Cocky Locky.

"I'm going to tell the king the sky is falling," said Henny Penny.

"May I come with you?" asked Cocky Locky.

"Certainly," said Henny Penny.

They went along and they went along and soon
they met Ducky Daddles.

"Where are you going?" asked Ducky Daddles.

"We're going to tell the king the sky is falling,"
said Henny Penny and Cocky Locky.

"May I come with you?" asked Ducky Daddles.

"Certainly," said the others.

they went along

46

They went along and they went along and soon
they met Goosey Poosey.

"Where are you going?" asked Goosey Poosey.

"We're going to tell the king the sky is falling,"
said Henny Penny, Cocky Locky
and Ducky Daddles.

and they went along

"May I come with you?"
asked Goosey Poosey.

"Certainly," said the others.

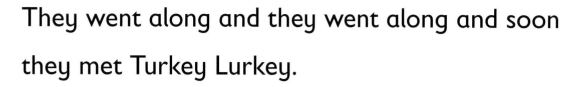

They went along and they went along and soon
they met Turkey Lurkey.
"Where are you going?" asked Turkey Lurkey.
"We're going to tell the king the sky is falling,"
said Henny Penny, Cocky Locky,
Ducky Daddles and Goosey Poosey.

"May I come with you?"
asked Turkey Lurkey.
"Certainly," said the others.

the sky is falling

soon they met
Foxy Woxy

They went along and they went along and soon
they met Foxy Woxy.

"Where are you going?" asked Foxy Woxy.

"We're going to tell the king the sky is falling,"
said Henny Penny, Cocky Locky, Ducky Daddles,
Goosey Poosey and Turkey Lurkey.

"But this is not the way to the king,"
said Foxy Woxy. "Let me show
you the way."

"Thank you," they said.

this is the way

Foxy Woxy led them to a dark and narrow hole.

"This is the way to the king," he said. "I'll go

first and you follow."

"Why of course, certainly, without doubt, why not?"

said Henny Penny, Cocky Locky, Ducky Daddles,

Goosey Poosey and Turkey Lurkey.

Turkey Lurkey went into the hole first.

CRUNCH! MUNCH!

Foxy Woxy bit off Turkey Lurkey's head.

hee hee hee

Goosey Poosey went into the hole next.

CRUNCH! MUNCH!

Foxy Woxy bit off Goosey Poosey's head.

Ducky Daddles went into the hole next.

CRUNCH! MUNCH!

Foxy Woxy bit off
Ducky Daddle's head.
Cocky Locky
went into the
hole next.
CRUNCH! Foxy Woxy
tried to bite off Cocky Locky's
head, but missed.
"Oh help!" cried Cocky Locky.
CRUNCH! MUNCH! Foxy Woxy did bite off his head.

oh help

Henny Penny heard Cocky Locky and she turned and ran home as fast as she could. So she never told the king the sky was falling.

Goldilocks and

Once upon a time there were three bears —
Daddy Bear, Mummy Bear and Baby Bear.
They lived in a cottage in a wood. Every morning
they made porridge for breakfast — a big bowl
for Daddy Bear, a medium-sized bowl for
Mummy Bear and a little bowl for Baby Bear.
One morning the porridge was very hot.
"Let's go for a walk while it cools down,"
Mummy Bear said. And off they went.

the three bears

While the three bears were out, a
little girl called Goldilocks came to
the cottage. She went straight inside.
"Oh look, lovely porridge!" she said.
She was very hungry.
First she tried the porridge in the big bowl.
"Too hot," she said.
Then she tried the porridge in the
medium-sized bowl.
"Too salty," she said.

yummy

Then she tried
the porridge in
the little bowl.
"Just right,"
she said and
ate it all up.

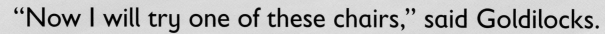
"Now I will try one of these chairs," said Goldilocks.

First she tried the big chair.

"Too hard," she said.

Then she tried the

medium-sized chair.

"Too soft," she said.

Crash

Then she tried the little chair.
"Just right," she said,
but when she sat on it,
CRACK! CRASH!
it broke into pieces.

Goldilocks was tired and wanted to lie down, so she went upstairs. First she tried the big bed. "Too high," she said. Next she tried the medium-sized bed. "Too lumpy," she said.

Then she tried the little bed.

"Just right," she said

and soon fell fast asleep.

Someone's been

eating my porridge

Before long the

three bears came home.

They looked at their bowls.

"Someone's been eating my porridge,"

said Daddy Bear.

"And someone's been eating my porridge,"

said Mummy Bear.

"And someone's been eating my porridge and

it's all gone," said Baby Bear.

someone's been sitting in my chair

68

Then the three bears looked at their chairs.

"Someone's been sitting in my chair,"

said Daddy Bear.

"And someone's been sitting in my chair,"

said Mummy Bear.

"And someone's been sitting in my chair

and now it's broken to bits," said Baby Bear.

Someone's been lying in my bed

Then the three bears went upstairs.

"Someone's been lying in my bed,"

said Daddy Bear.

"And someone's been lying in

my bed," said Mummy Bear.

"And someone's been lying in my bed," said Baby Bear.
"Look, there she is!"

look,

there she is

73

When Goldilocks woke up and saw the three bears, she jumped out of bed and out of the window and ran and ran away from the cottage.

The three bears never saw Goldilocks again.

75

The little red hen

Once upon a time
there was a little red hen,
who lived with a dog,
a goose and a cat.
One day the
little red hen
found some
grains of wheat.
"Who will help me plant
this wheat?" she asked.

"I'm busy," said the dog.

"I'm busy," said the goose.

"I'm busy," said the cat.

"Then I shall plant it myself," she said.

And she did.

Every day the little red hen watered and
weeded the ground, until tiny shoots appeared.
Slowly the shoots grew tall and strong and
then one day the wheat was ready for cutting.

I'm busy

"Who will help me cut the wheat?" asked the little red hen.

I'm busy

I'm busy

81

The wheat was ready to be taken to the mill,

to be ground into flour.

"Who will help me take the wheat to the mill?"

asked the little red hen.

"I'm busy," said the dog.

"I'm busy," said the goose.

"I'm busy," said the cat.

"Then I'll take it myself," she said. And she did.

she took the wheat

to the mill

83

she
baked the
bread

84

The little red hen brought the flour back home.

Now it was time for baking.

"Who will help me bake the bread?"

asked the little red hen.

"I'm busy," said the dog.

"I'm busy," said the goose.

"I'm busy," said the cat.

"Then I'll bake it myself,"

she said. And she did.

When the little red hen took the bread

out of the oven, it smelled delicious.

"Who will help me eat the bread?"

asked the little red hen.

"I will," said the dog.

"I will," said the goose.

"I will," said the cat.

"Oh no you won't," said the little red hen

and she ate it all up herself.

The

three little pigs

Once upon a time there was a mother pig with three little pigs. They were so poor that the mother pig sent the little pigs away to seek their fortune.

The first little pig
met a man with a
bundle of straw.
"Please, Man," he said,
"give me that straw to
build a house."
Which the man did and
the little pig built his house.

please, Man

Then along came a wolf who knocked at the door.

"Little Pig, Little Pig, let me come in."

The little pig answered, "No, no, by the hair
of my chinny chin chin!"

So the wolf said,

"Then I'll huff and I'll puff and

I'll blow your house in!"

And he huffed and he puffed and he blew the house in and ate up the first little pig.

The second little pig met a man

with a bundle of sticks.

please, Man

"Please, Man," he said, "give me those sticks to build a house." Which the man did and the little pig built his house.

Then along came the wolf and knocked at the door.

"Little Pig, Little Pig, let me come in."

The little pig answered,

"No, no, by the hair of my chinny chin chin!"

So the wolf said,

"Then I'll huff and I'll puff

and I'll blow your house in!"

And he huffed and
he puffed and he blew
the house in and ate up
the second little pig.

The third little pig met a man
with a load of bricks.
"Please, Man," he said,
"give me those bricks
to build a house."
Which the man did
and the little pig
built his house.

please, Man

huff puff

Then along came the wolf
and knocked at the door.
"Little Pig, Little Pig,
let me come in."
The little pig answered,
"No, no, by the hair of
my chinny chin chin!"
So the wolf said,
"Then I'll huff and I'll puff
and I'll blow your house in!"
And he huffed and he puffed,
but he could not blow
the house in.

The wolf was very angry.

"Little Pig," he said, "I'm going to climb

down your chimney and eat you up!"

So the little pig made a blazing fire and

put a huge pot of water on to boil.

grrrr

As the wolf was coming down the chimney, the little pig took the lid off the pot and the wolf fell in. The little pig put the lid back on and boiled up the wolf and ate him for supper.

The little pig lived happily ever after.

bye-bye wolf

The Musicians of Bremen

Once upon a time a donkey decided to go to Bremen to become a musician. On the way he met a sad dog. "What is the matter, Dog?" asked the donkey. "Nobody loves me," said the dog. "Come with me to Bremen and be a musician," said the donkey. "I'll play the guitar and you can play the drums." So on they went together along the road.

Soon they met a sad cat.
"What is the matter, Cat?"
asked the donkey.
"Nobody loves me,"
said the cat.
"Come with us to Bremen
and be a musician,"
said the donkey. "I'll play
the guitar, Dog will play
the drums and you can
play the violin."
So on they went together
along the road.

the matter?

Soon they met a sad cockerel.

"What is the matter, Cockerel?" asked the donkey.

"Nobody loves me," said the cockerel.

"Come with us to Bremen and be a musician," said the donkey.

"I'll play the guitar, Dog will play the drums, Cat will

play the violin and you can sing."

So on they went along the

road until nightfall.

In the dark they came across a robbers' house.

Donkey peeped in through a window.

"What can you see?" asked Dog, Cat and Cockerel.

"Lots of food and a warm fire," said Donkey.

"What else?" asked the others.

"Four robbers eating their dinner," said Donkey.

The animals made a plan to chase out the robbers.

Donkey stood with his hooves against the window.

Dog stood on Donkey's back, Cat on Dog's back and

Cockerel on Cat's head. Then they made music.

Ee-aw, woof woof, miaow, cock-a-doodle-doo!

And they fell through the window with a mighty crash!

The robbers were so

frightened they

ran away.

Donkey, Dog, Cat and
Cockerel ate all the food.
Then they went to bed.

Donkey found some straw outside in the yard.

Dog lay behind the door.

Cat curled up by the fire.

Cockerel flew up on to the roof.

Soon they were fast asleep.

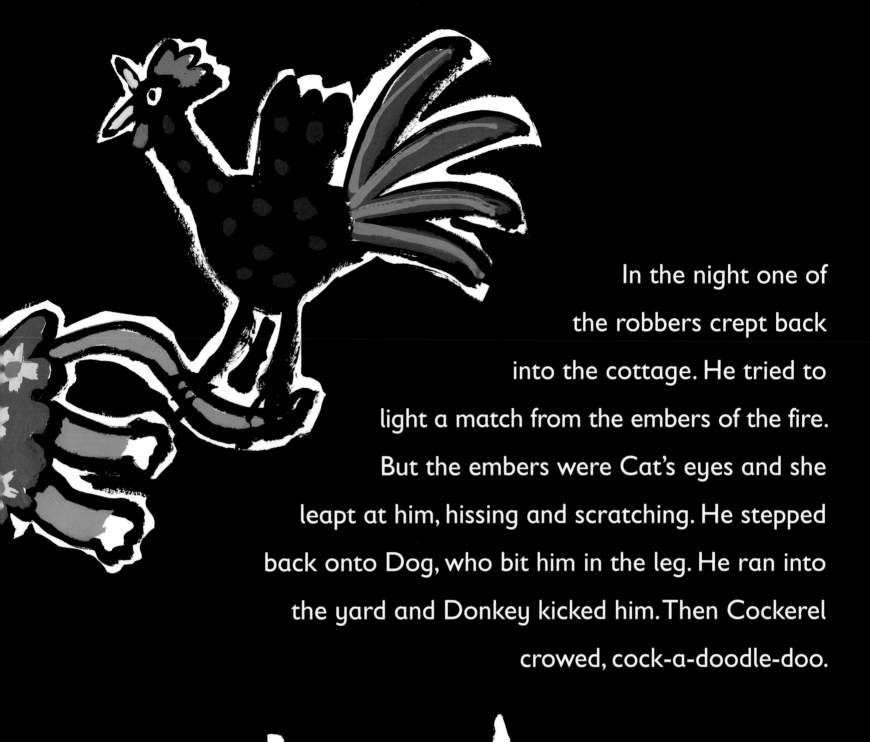

In the night one of
the robbers crept back
into the cottage. He tried to
light a match from the embers of the fire.
But the embers were Cat's eyes and she
leapt at him, hissing and scratching. He stepped
back onto Dog, who bit him in the leg. He ran into
the yard and Donkey kicked him. Then Cockerel
crowed, cock-a-doodle-doo.

help

The robber ran back to his friends.

"There's a witch in the house who scratched my face," he cried. "And there's a man with a knife who stabbed me in the leg. And there's a monster in the yard who beat me with a club. And there's a judge up above, who shouted, 'I'll lock you up, you rascal, you!'"

The robbers were so scared they never came back again.

And Donkey, Dog, Cat and Cockerel

never went to Bremen,

but lived happily ever after

in the cottage.